How Do You Read to a Rabbit?

Andrea Wayne von Königslöw

annick press
toronto + new york + vancouver

For my three bunnies, Alexis, Taika, and Kier, and my husband Rainer ...
and thanks to Sheryl, David, and EVERYONE in the Annick family.
—A.W.vK.

Everyone likes a bedtime story.
But have you ever tried to
read to an animal?

If you read a bedtime story to a hippopotamus, he might want to sit on your lap.

Can you read aloud to a kangaroo? No! She'll want you to jump around far too much.

You can try to read to dolphins,
but your words would get all wet.

And why can't you
read a book to owls?
Because they'll keep
asking ... whooo????

You can choose a good book for an alligator, but don't let him get a taste for the story.

If you want to read to bunnies, you'll need books and books and books.

It's impossible to read to camels.
Their big humps always get in the way.

If you read a book to a boa, she might want to hug you goodnight.

Can you read a bedtime story to bats? It's not easy to read upside down.

If you read a book to chameleons, they might get lost in the story.

It's even harder to read to a cheetah.
You might not be a fast enough reader.

Why can't you read to giraffes?
They are too tall to see the pictures.

And forget about reading to a parrot.
He will just copy everything you say.

But you CAN read to
your mom and dad.
It will be the best
story that they've
ever heard.

©2010 Andrea Wayne von Königslöw (text and illustrations)
Design: Sheryl Shapiro

Annick Press Ltd.

We acknowledge the support of the Canada Council for
the Arts, the Ontario Arts Council, and the Government of
Canada through the Book Publishing Industry Development
Program (BPIDP) for our publishing activities.

ONTARIO ARTS COUNCIL
CONSEIL DES ARTS DE L'ONTARIO

Cataloging in Publication

Von Königslöw, Andrea Wayne
       How do you read to a rabbit? / written and
illustrated by Andrea Wayne von Königslöw.

ISBN 978-1-55451-232-4 (bound).—ISBN 978-1-55451-231-7 (pbk.)

       I. Title.

PS8593.056H69 2010   jC813'.54   C2009-905761-1

The art in this book was rendered in watercolor.
The text was typeset in Zemke Hand ITC.

Distributed in Canada by: Published in the U.S.A. by:
Firefly Books Ltd.   Annick Press (U.S.) Ltd.
66 Leek Crescent   Distributed in the U.S.A. by:
Richmond Hill, ON   Firefly Books (U.S.) Inc.
L4B 1H1   P.O. Box 1338
                                 Ellicott Station
                                 Buffalo, NY 14205

Printed in China.

Visit Annick at: www.annickpress.com

Win an original drawing by Andrea Wayne von Königslöw!

The fun doesn't stop here!

What other animals can you think of that would enjoy a story, and why
might reading to them be difficult? For example, "You can try to read to
a lion, but you would have to shout loud enough to drown out its roar."

Submit your idea(s), and if we pick your name, Andrea Wayne von
Königslöw will send you a signed, original sketch based on your winning
entry. A selection of entries will be posted online (accompanied by your
first name only) at www.annickpress.com.

To enter, please visit www.annickpress.com/contests for full contest details!